1812

A SURPRISE FOR
Caroline

By KATHLEEN ERNST

ILLUSTRATIONS ROBERT PAPP

VIGNETTES LISA PAPP

★ American Girl®

THE AMERICAN GIRLS

1764 KAYA, an adventurous Nez Perce girl whose deep love for horses and respect for nature nourish her spirit

1774 FELICITY, a spunky, spritely colonial girl, full of energy and independence

1812 CAROLINE, a daring, self-reliant girl who learns to steer a steady course amid the challenges of war

1824 JOSEFINA, a Hispanic girl whose heart and hopes are as big as the New Mexico sky

1853 CÉCILE AND MARIE-GRACE, two girls whose friendship helps them—and New Orleans— survive terrible times

1854 KIRSTEN, a pioneer girl of strength and spirit who settles on the frontier

1864  ADDY, a courageous girl determined to be free in the midst of the Civil War

1904  SAMANTHA, a bright Victorian beauty, an orphan raised by her wealthy grandmother

1914  REBECCA, a lively girl with dramatic flair growing up in New York City

1934  KIT, a clever, resourceful girl facing the Great Depression with spirit and determination

1944  MOLLY, who schemes and dreams on the home front during World War Two

1974  JULIE, a fun-loving girl from San Francisco who faces big changes—and creates a few of her own

Published by American Girl Publishing
Copyright © 2012 by American Girl

Questions or comments? Call 1-800-845-0005, visit **americangirl.com**,
or write to Customer Service, American Girl, 8400 Fairway Place,
Middleton, WI 53562-0497.

Printed in China
12 13 14 15 16 17 LEO 10 9 8 7 6 5 4 3 2 1

Deep appreciation to Constance Barone, Director, Sackets Harbor Battlefield
State Historic Site; Dianne Graves, historian; James Spurr, historian and First Officer,
Friends Good Will, Michigan Maritime Museum; and Stephen Wallace, former
Interpretive Programs Assistant, Sackets Harbor Battlefield State Historic Site.

Cataloging-in-Publication Data available from the Library of Congress

FOR BARBARA, WHO TRAVELED
TO HISTORIC SITES WITH ME,
AND FOR STEPHANIE,
WHO WENT TO WORK WITH ME

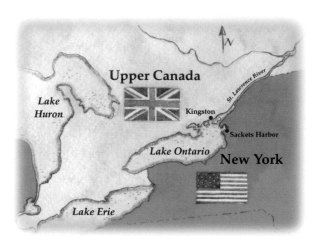

Caroline Abbott is growing up in Sackets Harbor, New York, right on the shore of Lake Ontario. Just across the lake is the British colony of *Upper Canada*.

In 1812, the nation of Canada didn't exist yet. Instead, the lands north of the Great Lakes were still a collection of British colonies. Today, Upper Canada is the Canadian province of Ontario.

In Caroline's time, there was a colony called *Lower Canada*, too. It stretched from Upper Canada eastward to the Atlantic Ocean. Today, it's the province of Quebec.

TABLE OF CONTENTS

CAROLINE'S FAMILY AND FRIENDS

CAROLINE'S FAMILY

PAPA
Caroline's father, a fine shipbuilder who has been taken prisoner by the British

MAMA
Caroline's mother, a firm but understanding woman

CAROLINE
A daring girl who wants to be captain of her own ship one day

GRANDMOTHER
Mama's widowed mother, who makes her home with the Abbott family

LYDIA
Caroline's twelve-year-old cousin, whose family recently escaped from Upper Canada

RHONDA HATHAWAY

*A twelve-year-old girl from the
big city of Albany who boards
at the Abbotts' house*

AMELIA HATHAWAY

*Rhonda's four-year-old sister,
who is also boarding
with the Abbotts*

MR. TATE

*The chief carpenter at
Abbott's and a good friend
of Caroline's family*

HOSEA BARTON

*A skilled sailmaker at
Abbott's Shipyard*

WINTER WISHES

Caroline Abbott held up two pieces of cloth. "Shall we use this brown cotton for the doll's dress?" she asked. "Or the blue silk?"

Lydia Livingston, Caroline's cousin, pointed at the blue fabric. "Let's use that beautiful silk!"

"I don't know if that's wise," said Rhonda Hathaway. The three girls were making the doll to give to Rhonda's little sister for Christmas. "Amelia doesn't always take care of things as well as she should. Perhaps the brown fabric would be better. It's sturdier, and it won't show dirt."

"What do you think, Caroline?" Lydia asked.

Caroline was pleased by the question. She was

1

a couple of years younger than Lydia and Rhonda, and they didn't always ask her opinion. "If we give Amelia a doll wearing a pretty party dress," she said, "I think she'll take good care of it."

Rhonda tipped her head thoughtfully. "You may be right. Yes. Let's use the blue silk."

Without warning, the door opened and Amelia, who was four years old, peeked inside. Her face brightened when she saw the older girls. "What are you doing?" she asked as Lydia quickly hid the doll behind her back.

"Amelia!" Rhonda scolded. "You mustn't enter a room without knocking. Go away."

Amelia's smile faded. "Why can't I come in?" she asked. Her face puckered as if she was about to cry.

Caroline jumped up and led Amelia back into the hall. She couldn't tell Amelia that she'd almost ruined her own Christmas surprise! "We—we're busy with something, that's all."

"Everyone's always busy." Amelia thrust out her lower lip in a pout. "I just want someone to play with me!"

I wish Amelia had children near her own age to play with, Caroline thought. She crouched down so that she could look Amelia in the eye. "I'm sorry, but we can't start any games now. Rhonda and Lydia and I will leave for lessons soon. Why don't you go ask my grandmother if she needs help in the kitchen?"

Caroline waited until Amelia had plodded downstairs before going back into the bedroom. "She's gone," Caroline reported.

"It will be hard to keep this doll a secret until Christmas!" Rhonda said. "We'd better finish our planning now." She draped the blue cloth around the doll as if imagining the dress. "I'll make some lace trim."

"And I've got an old glove we can cut up to make shoes," Caroline added. "Amelia shall have the prettiest doll in New York State!"

Lydia pulled some white cloth from the pile of scraps. "We'll need to make the doll a petticoat."

"Two petticoats," Rhonda said.

"If it were up to you, we'd make six petticoats," Lydia teased. "You're always cold!"

Rhonda laughed, fingering the scraps. "Caroline, I'm glad you suggested that we make this gift for Amelia. She'll be so pleased."

"I know Amelia wasn't able to bring any toys

with her when you moved here," Caroline said sympathetically. Rhonda and Amelia's father, an army officer, had been sent to Sackets Harbor after the United States declared war on Great Britain. His wife and daughters had come too, and had moved into the Abbotts' house.

"We couldn't bring much with us," Rhonda agreed. She looked at Lydia. "We were able to carry more than your family could, though. I can't imagine having to sneak away from home in the dead of night, as you did!"

Several weeks earlier, Lydia and her parents had fled Upper Canada, which was controlled by the British, and had squeezed into Caroline's house as well. "It *was* scary," Lydia admitted. "But we made it here safely. And as soon as my father finds a new place to farm, we'll start over again." She lifted her chin, as if facing a big challenge she was determined to win. "I'm glad we'll be here for Christmas, though."

"And since Christmas is just a week away," Rhonda reminded them, "we'll need to work quickly to finish this gift."

The reminder that Christmas was approaching made Caroline feel both excited and anxious. She had hemmed new handkerchiefs for her mother, her grandmother, her aunt and uncle, and Mrs. Hathaway. She'd secretly sewn a warm winter muff for Lydia, too. But she still didn't have a Christmas gift for Rhonda! Rhonda already had a muff to warm her hands, and several handkerchiefs with her initials embroidered in silk. Try as she might, Caroline hadn't been able to think of a single good idea for her friend.

Well, at least I had a good idea for Amelia's gift, Caroline thought. She was sure that Amelia would love the doll. And it was great fun to sew the doll and plan her clothes with Rhonda and Lydia. She smiled at the other girls. "I can embroider a face on the doll," she said, "but what shall we use for hair?"

"When my mother knit mittens for Amelia, she had a little yarn left over," Rhonda said. "The yarn isn't dyed, though—it's just white. Do you think we might be able to color it?"

Lydia giggled. "You mustn't ask *Caroline* about dyeing yarn." She nudged Caroline in the ribs. "Remember when we were little, and you decided to dye yarn with pokeberries?"

"You helped," Caroline protested. "It wasn't all my fault."

5

"What wasn't your fault?" Rhonda asked.

"By the time we were finished, our hands were as purple as the yarn," Caroline confessed.

Lydia flopped down on the bed, laughing. "Our mothers scolded us, but we could tell that they thought it was funny."

Rhonda snickered. "It must have looked as if you both were wearing horrid purple gloves!"

Lydia held her arms in the air gracefully. "My dear Miss Hathaway," she said as if she were a fine lady, "purple gloves are the newest style! All the French ladies are wearing them."

"Oh, my," Rhonda said. "I am sorely behind the times."

Caroline pretended to look down her nose at Rhonda. "We shall show you *all* the latest fashions."

Rhonda got her giggles under control. "Perhaps we shouldn't dye the yarn for Amelia's doll."

"It will be *fine*," Caroline promised. "I'll ask Grandmother to help us this time."

Someone knocked on the door. Caroline thrust the doll beneath her pillow.

Mrs. Hathaway stepped inside. "Gracious!" she said. "I could hear you girls laughing from downstairs.

It's almost time for your lessons. Tidy up your sewing, and then you may be off to the shipyard."

There was no school in Sackets Harbor, so Caroline's mother sometimes gave the three girls lessons. Since Mama was busy managing Abbott's Shipyard, the girls gathered in the office there, huddling by the stove in one corner.

"Ready for the last arithmetic problem?" Mama asked.

The girls nodded.

"Listen carefully," Mama said. "A captain loads a ship with a barrel of whale oil that weighs two hundred and sixty pounds, a barrel of salt that weighs ninety-five pounds, and a barrel of fish that weighs one hundred and fourteen pounds. How many pounds are in the ship's hold?"

Caroline carefully wrote *260, 95,* and *114* in a column on her slate. Since she dreamed of being captain of her own ship one day, she liked this type of problem. She began to add the numbers.

"Finished!" Rhonda declared.

Lydia put her slate pencil down. "Me too!"

"Let's give Caroline another moment," Mama said.

Caroline bent her head over her slate, trying to concentrate. Finally she wrote her answer. The little slate pencil made a scratchy sound.

"All right," Mama said. "What is the total?"

Lydia and Rhonda spoke at the same time. "Four hundred and sixty-nine."

Oh no, Caroline thought as she reluctantly displayed her slate. She'd written *369* at the bottom.

"You forgot to carry the one, Caroline," Mama said.

Lydia handed Caroline a rag. She rubbed the mistake from her slate. The warm feeling she'd had when the three girls had been planning Amelia's doll together was gone now. The error reminded Caroline that she was younger than Lydia and Rhonda. *It probably reminds them of that, too,* she thought.

"Very well, girls," Mama said. "That's all for today." She opened the stove door and added a log to the fire.

"I can tutor you in arithmetic, if you'd like," Rhonda told Caroline.

"It's kind of you to offer," Caroline said, trying to be polite without actually agreeing. She walked to the window and rubbed some frost from the glass so that she could peek outside. The fierce wind rattled the window and swirled snow in the air. She could barely make out the ships frozen into the harbor. As soon as the weather cleared, though, she knew that villagers would be outside with sleds, snowshoes, sleighs—*and best of all,* Caroline thought, *ice skates!* Her spirits rose. She couldn't wait to be flying across the ice.

Behind her, Mama handed Lydia and Rhonda their cloaks. "Be sure to wrap up well," Mama said.

Rhonda shivered as she put on her bonnet. "Winter is harsh here by the lake."

"We've just had a run of bad weather," Caroline told her. For the past few weeks, they'd had nothing but bitter cold, blinding blizzards, and howling winds. "Winter can be great fun. You'll see!"

Lydia pulled on her thick woolen mittens. "Are you coming with us, Caroline?" she asked.

"I'll be along later," Caroline replied. "I'm going to help Mama for a while."

Standing at the window, Caroline watched

Rhonda and Lydia head for home, leaning close and chattering together. Caroline sighed. "Rhonda and Lydia are better at sums than I am."

"They're also older than you are," Mama said gently. "You're doing well for someone who just turned ten."

"But I'm always the last to finish!" Caroline said.

Mama smoothed a strand of hair away from Caroline's forehead. "You're not used to having other students in class. I hope the fun of having two friends staying with us makes up for that."

"I do like having Rhonda and Lydia with us," Caroline said. "But sometimes . . . sometimes it feels as if Lydia and Rhonda are better friends with each other than they are with me."

"I'm sure that's not true," Mama said. She handed Caroline a small glass bottle of ink that had frozen overnight. "Now, please put this by the stove so that it can thaw while we eat."

Caroline and Mama shared a midday meal of baked beans and cornbread, brought from home in a tin bucket. When Mama went back to work, Caroline swept the office. Then she noticed that the woodbox was almost empty. She bundled up and went outside.

The shipyard was noisy and bustling as the men worked at top speed to build ships for the navy. Today two crews were sawing logs into planks with a *whizz-whizz* sound.

Caroline smiled proudly. The workers had recently finished one gunboat, and they were already starting the next. Soon the new boat would take shape, right over there—

Caroline caught her breath. She could see clearly across the yard. The wind was no longer blowing snow about. Such fine, calm weather meant it was safe to go skating!

Caroline darted back into the office. "Mama, may I go skating?" She bounced on her toes. "Please? I'll ask Lydia and Rhonda to come along." Skating was surely something that all three of them could enjoy together!

"You may," Mama said. Then she gave Caroline a stern look. "As long as the other girls go with you, that is. Remember the rule."

"I won't forget," Caroline promised. She was not permitted to go out on the frozen lake by herself.

Caroline hurried home as fast as the drifted snow allowed. As she ran upstairs, she heard Lydia's and Rhonda's voices coming from her bedchamber. Caroline burst into the room. "The wind has died!" she announced.

"Thank goodness," Lydia said. She was holding Caroline's little mirror, watching as Rhonda arranged her hair.

"Mmm," Rhonda added. She had a hairpin pinched between her lips. She used it to pin a curl in place on top of Lydia's head.

Didn't the older girls understand? "That means we can go out on the lake," Caroline said.

"Why would we want to do that?" Rhonda asked.

"We can go skating!" Caroline explained happily.

"What do you think, Rhonda?" Lydia asked. "Shall we go skating?"

Caroline's smile slipped away. In the old days, the promise of sunshine and good ice would have made Lydia race Caroline out the front door.

"Not today, I don't think," Rhonda said. "I like fixing hair. I don't want to go outside in this cold anyway."

Lydia held out a picture of a woman wearing

stylish clothes. "Your neighbor loaned us a copy of *The Lady's Magazine*," she told Caroline. "Rhonda is arranging my hair so that I look like the lady in this illustration. See?"

"And then Lydia's going to arrange *my* hair," Rhonda added. "We'll do yours too, if you want."

Caroline's shoulders slumped. How could Lydia and Rhonda think that arranging hair was more fun than skating? "No, thank you," she said. With a sigh, she left the older girls alone and headed back downstairs.

Caroline found Grandmother sitting by the kitchen fire with a pile of mending. Grandmother peered at her. "You look troubled, child."

Caroline dropped onto a bench. "I wanted to go skating this afternoon," she said.

"Why don't you, then?" Grandmother asked.

Caroline thumped her heel against the bench. "Because Rhonda and Lydia won't go with me."

"Ah." Grandmother nodded. "I wish I could take you, Caroline, but my skating days are long behind me." A faraway look came into her eyes. "I was a fine skater in my day, though. What fun it is to glide over the ice!"

"Oh, *yes,*" Caroline said. She loved seeing sunlight glitter on ice. She loved breathing in the crisp, clean air. She loved flying over the frozen lake, free as a bird.

"Why don't you take Amelia sledding instead?" Grandmother asked. "I believe she's in the parlor with her mother."

Caroline sighed. "Amelia is too little to sled down a *real* hill," she told Grandmother. "I'd just have to pull her around. That wouldn't be any fun."

Grandmother looked down her nose at Caroline, then went back to her sewing.

That look made Caroline feel guilty. "I'll play with Amelia another time," she promised. "Today, I want to go skating with Lydia and Rhonda. But Rhonda doesn't want to." *And Rhonda's opinion seems to be more important to Lydia than my wishes,* Caroline couldn't help adding to herself.

Grandmother made a knot and snipped the thread. "Does Rhonda know how to skate?"

Caroline blinked. Didn't everyone know how to skate? "I...I didn't ask."

"Well, my girl," Grandmother said, "perhaps you should."

Caroline thought about that. Rhonda was new to Lake Ontario. Maybe she *didn't* know how to skate. *If that's true*, Caroline thought, *Lydia and I can teach her.* She grinned.

"Thank you, Grandmother," Caroline said. She already felt more cheerful. Soon she'd be out on the frozen lake with her friends—and for once, being the youngest wouldn't matter one bit.

CHAPTER
TWO
—

NOT LADYLIKE

Caroline ran out of the kitchen and back upstairs. In the bedroom, Rhonda was holding the mirror now. "Did you change your mind?" she asked. "Would you like us to fix your hair, too?"

"No, thank you," Caroline said. "Rhonda, do you know how to skate?"

Rhonda made a face. "I tried skating once. My ankles wobbled. I fell six times. I had bruises all over."

"Lydia and I can teach you!" Caroline offered.

Rhonda shook her head.

"Hold still!" Lydia cried. "Oh, I've made a snarl now. I need to comb it out and start over."

"Please, Rhonda?" Caroline asked. "Won't you try once more?"

"I don't have skates," Rhonda said.

Caroline had already thought of that. "You can borrow Mama's. They may be a little too big, but you can manage. It will be fun!"

"If the skates are too big, I'll be even more likely to fall." Rhonda sighed. "Besides, Caroline, we're already doing something fun."

Caroline's frustration popped out. "But it's silly to stay inside on such a sunny day!"

The room got quiet. Lydia and Rhonda exchanged a look in the mirror. Caroline waited, hoping one of them would say, *You're right, Caroline. It's a fine day for skating, and the three of us shouldn't waste it. Let's head out, all together.* But neither girl spoke. Finally Caroline turned around, left the room, and thumped down the stairs.

In the parlor, she went to the front window and looked out toward Lake Ontario. *Oh, Papa,* she thought, *where are you?* If Papa were here, *he* would understand how she felt.

The British had been holding Papa as a prisoner ever since the war began in June. Right now, the ache in Caroline's heart felt worse than ever. Papa loved to skate! He had taught Caroline when she was a little girl. On the first good day for skating the previous winter, Papa had been too busy to take Caroline out on the ice. After supper, however, he'd told her to fetch her skates.

"But, Papa, the sun has gone down!" Caroline had protested.

"So it has," Papa had said, his eyes twinkling. "The moon is full, though." And off the two of them had gone. It had been magical to skate in the hush of nighttime, with starlight glowing on the frozen lake and a bonfire blazing on shore to guide skaters home.

Caroline sighed, tucked that special memory away, and went back to the kitchen. "Rhonda doesn't know how to skate," she reported to Grandmother. "I said that Lydia and I could teach her, but she said no." Caroline dropped back on the bench. "That means I can't go."

Grandmother gave Caroline a look that seemed to say, *Come, Caroline, stop complaining. What are you going to do now?*

Caroline heard faint giggling from upstairs and glanced wistfully toward the sound. It would be so much fun to skate between Rhonda and Lydia! She imagined the three of them laughing and talking, maybe even racing each other back to the shore.

I know the three of us can have fun together, Caroline thought. Two days earlier the older girls had helped with Caroline's least favorite chore, baking bread. While scheming about Amelia's doll and giggling about flour on Lydia's nose, they'd made four tasty loaves. If they could enjoy a chore like baking, sharing winter games should be even better. Caroline stared at the fire. It shouldn't be so hard to convince the older girls to bundle up and head outdoors!

Well, I'm not giving up, she thought. They had a long winter ahead, and she wanted to enjoy it with Lydia and Rhonda.

"On days like this, I wish we could have lessons at home," Rhonda said the next morning as she bundled up to walk to the shipyard with Caroline and Lydia. "It's so cold!"

Caroline waved at a neighbor who was chopping firewood. "We just need to keep moving," she said. "At least it's sunny today." She liked the way sunshine flashed on the icicles hanging from every roof.

As the girls turned a corner, they heard shouts and laughter coming from a group of boys who were sledding down a hill. "Caroline!" one of them called. "Want to take a run?" He gestured to his sled.

"Yes!" Grinning, she turned to her companions. "Let's all go!"

Rhonda shook her head. Lydia hesitated before saying, "We really don't have time."

Caroline frowned. Lydia had always loved to go sledding! Caroline turned her back and hurried to the top of the hill. When the other girls saw how fast she went, perhaps they would change their minds.

"Watch me," Caroline called, settling on the sled. She dug her heels into the snow and pushed off. *Whoosh!* She laughed as the sled flew down the slope, the wind stinging her cheeks.

She was almost to the bottom of the hill before she saw that the boys had built up a wall of snow to keep sledders from zooming into the road. She leaned back and dug in her heels again, but she was going too fast to stop.

The sled crashed into the snowbank. Caroline flew from her sled. "Ooh!" she yelped as icy snow slid under her collar. She didn't mind getting a little snow down her neck, though. That ride was worth it.

"That was fun!" she called to the other girls. "Want to try?"

"It's time for lessons," Rhonda said.

Caroline gave the sled back to its owner and joined Rhonda and Lydia. "Mama won't mind if we're a few minutes late," she said. "Are you sure you don't want to take just one slide before we go to the shipyard?"

"Sledding isn't ladylike," Lydia said.

"You're covered with snow!" Rhonda added. "Gracious, Caroline."

Caroline brushed at her cloak with mittened hands. "It doesn't matter," she said. When had Lydia decided that she was too ladylike to go sledding? Why was Rhonda so worried about a tiny bit of snow?

"That was fun!" Caroline said. "Are you sure you don't want to take just one slide down the hill before we go to the shipyard?"

"We really must go," Lydia said. "Come along, Caroline." She turned away, and Rhonda followed.

Caroline kicked some snow. *Lydia sounds as if she's my mother,* she thought, *instead of my cousin!*

After lessons Caroline told the older girls, "I'm going to stay here at the shipyard and help the men unravel old rope to make caulk. Would you like to help?"

Lydia and Rhonda exchanged a glance. "I don't think so," Lydia said. "We'll see you at home later." Rhonda nodded.

Well, fine, Caroline thought crossly. *I'm going to stay and do something important.*

After sharing a noon meal with Mama, Caroline left the office. In the carpentry shop, she found Hosea, the sailmaker, sitting near a little stove. He was mending a torn piece of canvas. Jed, the youngest carpenter, was carving wooden pegs that would help hold the new gunboat together.

A third man, Richard, sat beside a mound of old

rope. "Come to help, Miss Caroline?" he asked.

"Yes," Caroline told him. She fetched an empty workbasket, picked up one of the pieces of rope, and settled on a little stool. Then she began picking the rope apart.

Richard was a caulker. His job was to seal boats so that not a drop of water could seep in. He made something called oakum from the loose strands of old rope. The oakum was mixed with sticky pitch from pine trees. Richard hammered the mixture into the tiny cracks between wooden planks. Caroline loved knowing that *her* bits of rope would become part of a gunboat that would fight the British.

She worked steadily, listening as the men swapped stories. Her thoughts kept straying to Rhonda and Lydia, though. *Unraveling rope is important work—but I suppose it's not **ladylike** enough for them,* Caroline thought.

"Are you looking forward to Christmas, Miss Caroline?" Richard asked.

Caroline nodded, but her spirits drooped even lower. The holiday was only a few days away, and she still needed a gift for Rhonda. Teaching her to skate would make a good gift... but Rhonda had already said she didn't want to try again.

Suddenly Caroline sat up straight, her hands going still. What if she could give Rhonda a pair of new skates for Christmas? Beautiful skates, just her size. Rhonda liked pretty things, and having skates that fit her well might encourage her to try again.

As Caroline reached for a piece of rope, another idea flashed through her mind. *Rope—that's it!* she thought. *I could tie a rope around Rhonda's waist and tow her across the ice.* Rhonda didn't want to skate because she was afraid of falling. But with someone towing her—

The door opened, and Mr. Tate stepped in with a blast of cold air. "How is the work coming?" he asked.

"Just fine," Hosea said.

"Miss Caroline's been a big help today," Richard added.

Mr. Tate nodded with approval at the mound of rope fibers between Caroline and Richard.

Caroline jumped to her feet. "Pardon me," she said, "but I was wondering..." Her voice trailed away. Mr. Tate had a lot of responsibility at the shipyard. Perhaps she shouldn't ask for special favors.

"Yes, Miss Caroline?" He gave her an encouraging smile. Mr. Tate had worked for Caroline's parents for many years. He was more than a worker—he was a family friend.

"I'd like to give Rhonda a pair of skates for Christmas," Caroline explained. "I know all the men are very busy, but I was wondering if—"

"Of course!" Mr. Tate understood at once. "It wouldn't take Joseph long to fashion the blades." Joseph was the blacksmith.

"And I could make the leather straps," Hosea offered. "I'll do it in the evening, sir," he added, looking at Mr. Tate.

Caroline clapped her hands. "Oh, *thank* you!" She beamed from one man to the other, bouncing on her toes. With a towrope, she was certain she could help Rhonda learn to glide over the ice. And she'd soon have a beautiful new pair of skates to give her friend on Christmas, too.

On the day before Christmas, someone knocked on the front door just as Caroline finished paring potatoes for Grandmother. Caroline opened the door. "Joseph, come in from the cold!" she said. Despite his warm wool coat and hat, the blacksmith's cheeks were bright red.

Joseph stamped snow from his shoes and stepped inside. He held a bulky canvas bundle under one arm. After greeting Grandmother, who was sitting by the fire, he said in a hoarse whisper, "I've got the skates, Miss Caroline."

"Ooh, let's see!" Caroline cried. "It's all right. Rhonda's off visiting her father today."

Joseph placed his bundle on the table and unwrapped a pair of skates.

Caroline's eyes widened. "Oh, *Joseph!*"

"I hope they suit," Joseph said. "Hosea and I worked from the tracing you made of Miss Rhonda's shoe, so the size should be just right."

Caroline examined the skates. The leather straps Hosea had made were soft and even. The blades Joseph had crafted were sharp and straight, and he'd added a fancy twist of iron on each toe. She looked from the delicate work to Joseph's huge hands and back again. "Those," she told him, "are surely the prettiest skates ever made."

"They are indeed," Grandmother agreed.

Joseph ducked his head, looking embarrassed. "I'm glad you think they'll do."

"Do?" Caroline grinned. "Rhonda is sure to love them!"

After bidding Joseph good-bye, Caroline picked up the skates. *At least . . . I hope Rhonda loves them,* she thought.

She took one last look at the skates before hiding them away in Grandmother's bedchamber. All Caroline could do now was wait to see if Rhonda was as delighted with the skates as *she* was.

CHRISTMAS

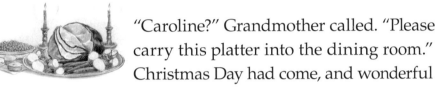

"Caroline?" Grandmother called. "Please carry this platter into the dining room." Christmas Day had come, and wonderful aromas had been drifting from the kitchen all day.

Caroline picked up the heavy platter and inhaled the rich scent of ham. For most of the year, only salted and smoked pork was available, but Grandmother had purchased a juicy fresh ham for Christmas dinner.

The dining room was crowded, but everyone managed to squeeze into place: Caroline, Mama, and Grandmother; Lydia, Aunt Martha, and Uncle Aaron; and Rhonda, Amelia, and their parents. All through the meal, the three older girls shared secret, excited looks. When Amelia saw the doll, would she be too surprised for words? Or would she chatter with excitement?

Caroline was confident that Amelia would like her gift. Would Rhonda be as happy with her beautiful new skates? Feeling hopeful, Caroline imagined Rhonda's face lighting with pleasure when she realized that Caroline had arranged to have them made just for *her*. Surely Rhonda wouldn't look down her nose and say "Gracious, Caroline!" then. Once Rhonda had her new skates and Lydia had the warm muff Caroline had made for her, there would be nothing to keep the three of them from having fun together on the ice.

Although Caroline had trouble sitting still, Christmas dinner was too wonderful to rush. Grandmother and Mrs. Hathaway served the ham with peas and potatoes. Aunt Martha had baked two apple pies and boiled cornmeal with sweet maple syrup to make hasty pudding.

After the feast, everyone moved into the parlor, and Uncle Aaron settled down with the Bible. This was the first time Papa hadn't been there to read the Christmas story, and Caroline felt a wave of longing as Uncle Aaron began. As she listened to the familiar words, she looked at the gift she'd made for Papa, an embroidered fire screen. It sat by the hearth, waiting to welcome him home. *Merry Christmas, Papa,* she thought, *wherever you are. I miss you more than ever.*

When Uncle Aaron finished, he shut the Bible gently. For a moment everyone was quiet, as if tucking the comforting story into their hearts for another year. Then Caroline tiptoed to Mama. "May we give our gifts now?" she asked.

Mama smiled. "Of course, dear child."

Lydia and Rhonda jumped to their feet. The three girls had decided that Amelia's gift would be the first one given.

Rhonda's face glowed with anticipation. "Close your eyes, Amelia," she said, "and hold out your hands. No peeking!"

Amelia scrunched her eyes tightly shut and eagerly held out her hands. Lydia fetched the doll from its hiding place in a drawer. She, Rhonda, and Caroline crowded close to gently lay the doll in Amelia's hands.

Amelia's eyes flew open. *"Oh,"* she gasped. She stared at the doll as if she'd never seen one before.

"Happy Christmas," Caroline said.

Amelia didn't move, keeping the doll balanced on her palms. "She's for *me*?" she asked.

Lydia laughed, clearly delighted by Amelia's wonderment. "She is," she assured the little girl. "The three of us made her just for you."

Slowly, gently, Amelia cradled the doll close. "She's *beautiful*."

"You must be careful with her," Rhonda added.

"I will," Amelia promised. "Thank you!" She put the doll down long enough to give each of the older girls a hug. When Caroline felt Amelia's arms squeeze her around the waist, her heart almost overflowed. She'd never seen Amelia so happy. The glance she shared with Lydia and Rhonda was full of satisfaction. *We did that,* Caroline thought. *With a good idea and a few scraps of cloth and yarn, we made Amelia happy.*

Then Amelia ran around the room, showing her new doll to the adults. "You girls did a lovely job," Mama said.

Mrs. Hathaway nodded. "You did indeed,"

*Slowly, gently, Amelia cradled the doll close. "She's **beautiful**."*

she agreed. "Even dyeing yarn that pretty shade of brown to make the hair."

Rhonda shared a secret smile with Caroline and Lydia. "Better brown than purple," she whispered.

Caroline tried not to giggle, but she couldn't help it. Lydia elbowed her, which was her cousin's way of saying, *Stop it! Don't make me laugh too!*

"Be polite, girls," Grandmother said, but her eyes were twinkling.

Amelia cradled her doll while more gifts were presented. Lydia sighed with delight when she saw her new muff. "It's so soft and warm!" she told Caroline. "Thank you."

Caroline took a deep breath. *I hope Rhonda is as happy with her gift as Amelia and Lydia are with theirs*, she thought. She felt tingly inside, half nervous and half excited. "I have a gift for you as well," Caroline told Rhonda. "Close your eyes."

Caroline fetched the skates from their hiding place and set them in Rhonda's lap. Rhonda opened her eyes. She stared at the skates.

"Hosea and Joseph made them," Caroline told her. "They're just the right size for you. Aren't they beautiful?"

Rhonda nodded.

"I know you didn't enjoy skating when you tried it before," Caroline added quickly, "but I think I can help keep you from falling."

"Thank you," Rhonda said finally. And that was all.

Caroline felt her heart slide toward her toes.

As the evening went by, Caroline received gifts of embroidery silk, a new needle case, and warm woolen stockings. When she passed out the handkerchiefs she'd made, the adults all praised her handiwork. "I was in sore need of a new handkerchief," Uncle Aaron declared.

Rhonda, however, wouldn't meet her gaze at all. And when Caroline looked at Lydia, her cousin quickly glanced away, as if embarrassed for her.

Caroline blinked, trying not to cry. Christmas was ruined.

That night Caroline lay in bed, listening to the two older girls whisper from their cornhusk mattresses on the floor nearby. *Perhaps I should*

forget about having fun with them, Caroline thought miserably.

She wished she'd explained her towrope plan when she presented the skates. Surely that would have put Rhonda's fears to rest! Maybe Rhonda loved the new skates but didn't show it because she was still afraid of falling. As Caroline finally drifted off to sleep, she knew what she needed to do.

The morning after Christmas dawned clear and cold. After breakfast, Caroline found Lydia and Rhonda in the parlor. "Mama has excused us from lessons today," Caroline began. "And it's a perfect morning for skating." She quickly explained her plan.

"You want to tow me over the ice?" Rhonda asked. "I don't think that will keep me from falling."

"No, wait," Lydia said thoughtfully. "It might work."

Caroline gave her cousin a grateful smile before turning back to Rhonda. "Getting started is the hardest part of learning to skate," she told her. "Getting a tow will help you build up speed."

Rhonda twisted her fingers together. "I don't know," she said.

"Skating really is great fun," Lydia told Rhonda.

"With a little practice, you'll glide all over the ice."

"Please, Rhonda?" Caroline said. "Will you give skating one more try?"

"Oh, very well," Rhonda said reluctantly. "I'll try."

The girls dressed in their warmest clothes, gathered up their skates, and walked to the harbor. Lots of other people were already skating on the frozen lake—some hesitant, others with great speed and grace. A few skated near the navy ships, but Caroline didn't want to go there. Sailors had chopped trenches in the ice around their ships so that spies or enemy soldiers couldn't walk across the frozen lake and sneak aboard. *We mustn't take Rhonda anywhere near open water,* she thought.

"Let's go over there," she said, pointing to an area that was well away from the ships and most of the other skaters.

"Are you sure the ice is safe?" Rhonda asked.

"Yes," Caroline said firmly. "Bad ice looks dark. Thick ice has a nice white color, like this. See?"

Then she pointed toward a man and woman using a chair sled nearby. The man was skating and pushing his sweetheart along while she sat on the sled. "That chair sled is a lot heavier than we are, and the ice is holding them up," she added.

"I've even seen horse-drawn sleighs pass through here." Lydia smiled reassuringly.

Rhonda squared her shoulders. "All right, then. I'm ready."

Caroline and Lydia strapped on their own skates and helped Rhonda put on hers. "Before you start, watch how I do it," Caroline told her friend. She pushed off on the ice. With just a few strokes, she felt as if she were flying!

Before going too far, though, she slowed reluctantly and returned to shore. "See?" she said to Rhonda. "You'll soon be skating like that too."

Caroline had borrowed a rope from the shipyard. While Lydia tied one end around Rhonda's waist, Caroline knotted the other end around her own. Lydia and Caroline helped Rhonda to her feet. Then they slowly moved onto the ice.

"My ankles are shaking already," Rhonda said.

"Hold on to my arm," Lydia offered. "Caroline, start pulling!"

Caroline pushed off on one foot. *"Oof,"* she gasped as the towrope tightened around her waist.

Towing Rhonda was harder than she'd expected.

She wasn't about to give up, though. She dug the blade of one skate into the ice and shoved off harder. That sent her forward a few inches. She pushed off again with her other foot.

"Faster!" Lydia called.

I'm trying, Caroline thought. Summoning every bit of her strength, she kept skating forward. They all began to move a little more quickly.

Lydia tried to encourage Caroline and Rhonda. "That's the way!"

Caroline clenched her teeth and chanted silently, *Push off with the left foot, push off with the right.* The ice had some bumps, but she tried to avoid them. Gradually, as she picked up speed, it grew a little easier to keep skating.

"I'm doing it!" Rhonda exclaimed. "I'm really skating!"

Rhonda sounded so happy that Caroline dared a look over her shoulder. Rhonda was taking little strokes herself. "Isn't this fun?" Caroline called. Rhonda nodded.

Caroline looked ahead again—and saw a ridge in the ice, right in front of her. She gave a little hop, easily clearing the rough spot, but she knew that Rhonda wasn't ready to make such a move. "Watch out!" Caroline yelled.

Too late! Rhonda tripped and fell, pulling Lydia down with her. Caroline felt a hard jerk on the rope. She banged down on the ice and slid backward into the other girls.

"Ow," Rhonda whimpered. She sat up slowly, rubbing her left elbow. Caroline was horrified to see tears in Rhonda's eyes.

"I'm sorry!" Caroline cried. "There was a bump in the ice, and I didn't see it in time. Next time I will—"

"No," Rhonda said. She pulled off her gloves and began fumbling with her skates. "I tried, Caroline. Just as I promised. But I *told* you I didn't think this would work. I don't want to fall down any more. I shall walk back to shore."

Caroline looked at Lydia, hoping her cousin would say something to change Rhonda's mind. But Lydia didn't speak. Caroline silently untied the towrope. All three girls got to their feet.

Caroline struggled to hold frustration and disappointment inside. If only she'd spotted the ridge in time! Perhaps if she had, Rhonda wouldn't have

*"Watch out!" Caroline yelled. Too late! Rhonda tripped and fell,
pulling Lydia down with her.*

fallen. *And if Rhonda hadn't fallen,* Caroline thought, *we all could have had fun on the lake.*

Caroline felt a heaviness settle in her heart as she took one last, longing look toward the other skaters skimming over the ice. She'd hardly gotten to skate at all!

Even worse, Rhonda was clearly more unhappy with Caroline than ever.

When Caroline entered her bedchamber that evening, she found Rhonda and Lydia in their nightgowns, brushing their hair. Caroline tried not to look at the beautiful skates she'd given Rhonda, which had been dropped in a corner.

A fierce wind seemed determined to sneak in around the windowpanes. *"Brrr!* I'm going to sleep in my shawl tonight," Lydia said. She wrapped her woolen shawl around her shoulders and quickly slid beneath her blankets.

Rhonda did the same thing, and once she was settled, she pulled her blanket up to her chin. "I wish it were spring," she said.

Caroline, busy undressing, didn't answer. If Rhonda was going to be unhappy until spring came, she'd be unhappy for a long time.

"It's so nice to be outside in warm weather," Rhonda continued. Her voice sounded dreamy and she closed her eyes, as if imagining herself into a fine spring day. "Back in Albany, my friends and I had tea parties outside, or we went to the green for hoop races."

"That sounds lovely," Lydia said wistfully.

"I like racing hoops too," Caroline said. She blew out the lamp and slid into bed. "Last year we had hoop races in the village on Independence Day." It had been great fun to roll big wooden hoops over the grass, while little children practiced nearby.

Suddenly, Caroline sat up as a new idea popped into her head. "We don't have to wait until spring to race hoops. We could race hoops on the snow!"

"Oh, Caroline," Lydia said in that I'm-older-and-smarter-than-you tone that Caroline particularly disliked. "Hoops would just sink in the snow!"

"Today's sunshine made the snow melt a little," Caroline pointed out, "so there will likely be a glaze of ice over everything tomorrow. I know a hill just outside of town that would be perfect for hoop races!"

"But we don't have hoops," Rhonda said.

"We can borrow some from the shipyard," Caroline promised. "I've seen spare wheel rims in the blacksmith shop. So, what do you think?" She held her breath, hoping that Rhonda and Lydia wouldn't dismiss this idea too.

"I think we should try it!" Lydia agreed. Her voice had lost its bossy tone. She sounded excited.

Caroline waited for Rhonda to respond.

"Yes, that does sound like fun," Rhonda said finally. "And I won't have to worry about falling down."

Caroline snuggled back under the covers. She could hardly wait for morning.

CHAPTER
FOUR
—

DANGER ON THE ICE

The next day, after lessons with Mama, Caroline told Lydia and Rhonda to head home without her. "I'll be along shortly," she promised. "I need to see the blacksmith."

She found Joseph working at his forge, shaping hot iron into a tool. "Excuse me," Caroline said, staying a safe distance from the forge as Papa had taught her. "Might I borrow some cartwheel rims?" She pointed toward one of the shop's dim corners, which was cluttered with all sorts of stray metal pieces and tools.

Joseph lay down his hammer. "Whatever for?"

"Lydia and Rhonda and I want to have hoop races," Caroline explained.

"I've got two small ones," Joseph said. "You're welcome to borrow them."

Caroline collected the two narrow iron rims, each about waist-high, and headed for home. *We need three hoops,* she thought, *or it won't be any fun.* She tried to think. Suddenly she smiled. She knew where there was another hoop.

When she got home, Caroline headed for the family's storeroom, where Grandmother's spinning wheel sat among traveling trunks and old pieces of furniture. Grandmother hadn't had any wool to work with in months, so the spinning wheel was dusty. It was made almost entirely from wood, but it had a narrow iron rim to hold the wheel together. The unheated storeroom was so cold and dry that the wooden wheel had shrunk a little. When Caroline pulled on the iron rim, it easily slid from the wheel. She grinned. Perfect!

With the hoop in hand, Caroline hurried downstairs and joined the other girls. "I've got three hoops," she said triumphantly. "We're all set."

Once they left home, Caroline led the way down

the lane, away from the busiest streets. With so many new ships and forts and storehouses being built, men had cut trees all around the village. Logs, planks, and bricks were piled here and there, ready for work crews.

The girls took a footpath out of the village and soon arrived at a quiet, sloping meadow. "See?" Caroline said, her breath puffing white in the cold air. "There's a nice crust on the snow."

Lydia considered the slope. "We won't be able to run alongside our hoops in this snow," she said.

"I thought we could launch the hoops from the top of the hill," Caroline said. "We can all send our hoops down at the same time. The first hoop to reach the bottom is the winner." She pointed. The gentle slope stretched down to the lakeshore, but a fallen tree at the bottom—now covered with snow—would keep the hoops from rolling onto the ice.

"That's a good idea," Rhonda agreed. She pulled her scarf more snugly around her neck. "Ooh, that wind is chilly. I wish the sun were out today."

"We'll stay warm as long as we keep moving," Lydia promised. "Let's line up here, on the hilltop."

The three girls positioned their hoops. "Ready?" Rhonda called. "Go!"

Caroline sent her hoop sailing, but it quickly fell over. Keeping a hoop going on the slick slope was tricky!

"This is harder than racing hoops on grass," Lydia gasped as the girls trudged back up the hill after their third try.

"I almost had it," Caroline said. "Next time my hoop will surely reach the bottom."

"Perhaps," Rhonda said with a teasing smile, "but *my* hoop is going to beat yours!"

As Caroline positioned her hoop for the next launch, she paused to enjoy the cold air against her face and the sound of footsteps crunching on snow. Rhonda's cheeks were flushed pink, and her eyes sparkled. Lydia laughed as she struggled the last few steps to the starting line. *Finally!* Caroline thought. She wanted to cheer.

This time, Lydia's hoop rolled all the way to the bottom of the hill. It hit the fallen log and fell over. "I win!" she crowed.

"This time you do," Rhonda informed her, "but Caroline and I will catch up to you!"

Soon all three girls were able to keep their hoops rolling. "Let's start keeping count," Lydia suggested. "If your hoop hits that little rise first, you win a point."

For some time the count stayed close. Each girl had a chance to cheer as her hoop reached the target first. Slowly, though, Caroline fell behind.

It doesn't matter, she tried telling herself, but she couldn't help wanting to win—or at least catch up! After coming in last three times in a row, she paused at the top of the slope, thinking. She was using the hoop from the spinning wheel, which was not as heavy as the others. Perhaps she just needed to push her hoop harder.

"Ready?" Rhonda called again. "*Go!*"

Caroline launched her hoop with all her strength. The three hoops rolled down the slope, faster and faster. Caroline's hoop stayed out in front. "I'm going to win this time!" she cried. She clapped as her hoop sailed to the bottom.

Instead of falling over, though, the hoop kept spinning. It rolled right up the snow mound that covered the log. Then a gust of wind grabbed the hoop, carrying it over the rise and out of sight. Caroline's excitement turned to dismay as her hoop disappeared.

The three girls stared, open-mouthed. "My goodness!" Rhonda said.

They scrambled down the slope and over the log. Caroline stared at the frozen lake. "Where's the hoop?" she asked. "Do you see it?"

"No," Lydia said. Rhonda shook her head.

Caroline scanned the ice, looking this way and that. She couldn't see the iron hoop anywhere.

"The wind must have taken it a long way," Rhonda said at last.

Caroline lifted her chin. "Well then," she said, "we need to go out on the lake and look for it."

Lydia frowned. "Caroline, no! We don't know if the ice is safe here."

"I can tell if ice is safe," Caroline protested.

"*No*," Lydia said. "We're out of sight from the village. We mustn't go out there."

Caroline rubbed her mittened hands together anxiously. "I can't leave the hoop behind," she told the other girls. "It's the rim to Grandmother's spinning wheel."

Lydia's eyes went wide. "Did you ask permission before taking it?"

"No," Caroline admitted. "Do you think

Grandmother will be angry with us?"

"Perhaps you should have thought about that before taking her hoop," Lydia said. "Honestly, Caroline!"

"Stop scolding me!" Caroline burst out. "I wouldn't have taken the hoop if you two had been more friendly lately."

Lydia planted her hands on her hips. "This has nothing to do with Rhonda and me. You're the one who took the hoop."

"Stop it!" Rhonda cried. "Arguing won't help anything." She looked at Caroline. "You'll have to tell your grandmother what you did."

The other girls' scolding just made Caroline feel stubborn. "What I *have* to do," she retorted, "is find the hoop. It couldn't have gone too far."

"We're *not* going out on that ice," Rhonda insisted.

"I agree," Lydia added. "Listen, Caroline, we're older than you, and—"

"I don't care if you're older than me!" Caroline yelled. "I know how to read ice. I'm going to look for that hoop whether you like it or not."

Lydia and Rhonda exchanged a troubled glance.

"Are you coming with me?" Caroline demanded.

She stared at the other girls, daring them to say no.

No one spoke.

"Fine," Caroline said. "I'll go by myself." She turned away. Her hands were shaking, and her stomach felt upset. *But I can't change my mind now,* she thought. She turned her back, straightened her shoulders, and walked onto the ice.

Caroline hadn't taken more than three steps before Lydia said, "Caroline, wait. I'll come with you."

"Me too," Rhonda said with a heavy sigh.

Caroline blew out a long, relieved breath. "Thank you," she said with frosty politeness.

Looking over the lake, Caroline felt a whisper of unease. Was she doing the right thing? What would Papa think if he could see her now? She'd *thought* she was becoming the steady person Papa wanted her to be. She didn't feel that way now.

I made a mistake by taking the hoop without permission, Caroline thought, *but I'm trying to be responsible and bring it back. That **is** the right thing to do ... isn't it?* One thing was certain—she needed to remember everything Papa had taught her about safety on the frozen lake.

She turned and stepped back on the shore.

Then she poked among the trees until she found three long, stout sticks. She handed one to Rhonda. "Carry this so that it's even with the ice," she told Rhonda.

Rhonda looked confused. "Why?"

"Wind can shift the ice and cause cracks," Caroline explained. Seeing the look of alarm on Rhonda's face, she continued quickly, "But you usually have warning. When the ice cracks, it sounds like a pistol shot. If a crack *did* open in the ice and you fell through, the stick would catch on the ice and keep you from drowning."

"People hardly ever fall in," Lydia added, but she looked nervous. She took her stick. "Let's get started."

The girls stepped onto the ice. Caroline peered into the distance until her eyes ached. She could hardly tell where the ice ended and the sky began. Everything looked gray. *That hoop has to be out here somewhere,* she told herself. At least the ice was good—thick and white. The day was growing colder, though. Wind raced across the frozen lake. Caroline's fingers and toes were soon numb despite her thick woolen mittens and socks.

"We're getting awfully far from shore," Lydia said finally. "We should turn back—"

"I *see* it!" Caroline cried. "It's just ahead." She began to hurry.

Suddenly Lydia yelled, "*Stop!* The ice is broken up there!"

Looking up, Caroline saw that they were reaching the end of a solid ice shelf that stretched from shore. The hoop lay near the shelf's edge. Just beyond, big pieces of ice bobbed lightly. Jagged ribbons of open water appeared and disappeared between the cakes of ice as they jostled together.

Caroline swallowed hard, trying to read the ice as Papa had taught her. "I can still get the hoop."

"Caroline, do not go any farther," Lydia ordered. "I *forbid* you to take one more step."

"I'll be careful," Caroline protested.

Rhonda grabbed Caroline's arm. "Don't you dare," she said. "Lydia's right."

Caroline clenched her teeth. She was not going to permit Lydia and Rhonda to order her around— not when she was so close to the hoop! "I know what I'm doing," she insisted. "You two stay here. I'm the lightest."

Ignoring the other girls' warnings, Caroline began walking forward, step by careful step. She tapped the ice ahead of her with the stick, checking for any sign of weakness. She pushed her hat back, uncovering her ears even though they prickled with cold. If the ice cracked, she wanted to hear it.

One step. Another. One more. Caroline concentrated on her goal. Three more steps. She was there! Caroline stooped and grabbed the iron hoop. *I have it!* she thought triumphantly.

As she rose to her feet, an extra-sharp blast of wind almost knocked her back down. Then came a deafening *cra-a-acking* sound, loud as a gunshot. The ice lurched beneath Caroline's feet. She struggled to keep her balance.

"*Caroline!*" Lydia shrieked.

Caroline looked back toward shore and was horrified to see a narrow channel of water, black and threatening, open between her and the main ice shelf. She stood now on a loose piece of ice about the size of her bedroom floor.

"Can you jump over the water?" Rhonda cried.

"No," Caroline called fearfully. "This piece of ice is staying balanced because I'm right in the middle of it." If she moved toward the edge, her weight might tip the ice over—and she'd plunge into the freezing water.

Lydia and Rhonda began a conversation that Caroline couldn't hear, with lots of pointing and gesturing. Caroline knew that Lydia would keep Rhonda safe. Lydia knew as much about ice as Caroline did. *No, Lydia knows **more** than I do*, Caroline admitted miserably. She'd made a terrible decision. Now she was in terrible trouble.

She tried to think, but her brain felt like slush. Fear made it hard to breathe. What if the wind pushed all these loose pieces farther away from land? "Help me!" she pleaded, blinking back tears. "I don't know what to do!"

"Caroline!" Lydia called. "Crouch down."

For once, Caroline was very glad to get an order from her cousin. She obeyed.

Lydia continued, "Now, stretch out on your stomach."

Caroline slowly stretched out on the ice, gasping each time it wobbled beneath her. Despite her thick coat, lying on the ice sent a deeper chill into her bones.

On the main ice shelf, Lydia lay down in the same manner. Then she inched her way over the ice toward the crack. Rhonda held on to Lydia's ankles, ready to yank her back if the ice gave way.

Lydia stopped when she was near the edge of the ice shelf. Then she extended her stick slowly across the water and over the ice cake toward Caroline. "Grab the end!"

Caroline snaked her hand forward and grasped the end of Lydia's stick. "Don't try to pull me over," Caroline begged. "I'll fall into the water!"

"I'm just going to hang on," Lydia promised, "while Rhonda goes for help."

Knowing that Lydia was at the other end of the stick made Caroline feel a little better. At least she wasn't going to drift away.

As she watched Rhonda hurry off, Caroline tried to slow her racing heart. Lydia was in a bad spot too. What if the ice Lydia was lying on broke away as well? *Lydia is risking her own safety to help me,* Caroline thought with a new stab of fear. In fact, both Rhonda and Lydia had taken a great risk when they followed her onto the ice. Caroline felt tears brim over and freeze on her cheeks. She'd made many mistakes that day. No wonder the older girls didn't always listen to her ideas!

Caroline didn't know how long she lay shivering on the ice, clutching Lydia's stick, before she heard a distant shout. Rhonda appeared on the shore. But... she was alone! Caroline's hopes sank. Why hadn't Rhonda brought help?

Then she saw that Rhonda was dragging a long plank of wood. "I found a board," Caroline heard Rhonda say.

"Good," Lydia replied. "Lay it on the ice, and then slide it over the water to Caroline's piece of ice. Carefully!"

Rhonda placed the board on the ice shelf and gently pushed it forward. One end came to rest right beside Caroline.

"Caroline," Lydia called, "we'll hold down this end of the plank so you can walk across."

Moving as slowly and steadily as possible, Caroline began to rise to her feet. She had to let go of Lydia's stick so that she could use both arms to help keep her balance. Each time the ice bobbed beneath her, she caught her breath. Finally she was standing upright, but although the plank rested right beside her boots, she couldn't seem to take a step.

Caroline looked at her cousin. "What if the plank pushes my cake of ice underwater?"

"It won't," Lydia promised.

With a deep breath, Caroline stepped onto the board. It was very narrow. She took one last glance at the hoop. She wanted to grab it, but she was afraid that carrying it might throw her off balance.

Caroline began to walk along the plank, placing each foot carefully. Her legs trembled with cold and fright. She waved her arms wildly to keep from falling off the board.

When she reached the channel that had opened in the ice and saw the dark water moving restlessly below her, she froze with terror. If she lost her balance, she'd fall into Lake Ontario. The icy water would soak her heavy clothing, making it impossible for her to swim. Her hands would be too numb to grab Lydia's stick. The older girls wouldn't be able to save her.

"Almost there!" Lydia called.

Rhonda added, "You can do it, Caroline!"

Their encouragement gave Caroline the strength she needed to take another step. *Keep going*, she told

Keep going, *Caroline told herself.* Don't look down. Just keep going.

herself. *Don't stop moving. Don't look down. Just keep going.*

It seemed to take forever to inch over the open water. Finally Caroline moved past the channel. She'd reached the ice shelf. She was safe.

FAST FRIENDS

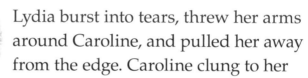

Lydia burst into tears, threw her arms around Caroline, and pulled her away from the edge. Caroline clung to her cousin as they walked toward the shore. Now that she was safe, she couldn't stop shaking.

"I was so frightened!" Lydia cried.

"I thought we'd lost you," Rhonda added, her voice cracking.

Caroline stepped back and looked from one girl to the other. "Th-thank you," she said through chattering teeth. "And—I'm s-sorry. I know I put us all in danger. I should never have gone out on the ice."

"We tried to say so," Lydia reminded her. "Why didn't you listen?"

It was hard to tell the truth, but Caroline knew she had to try. "Sometimes you two treat me like a little child," she said. "You never think about what *I* want to do. It makes me feel left out."

"*We* don't leave you out," Rhonda protested. "When we invite you to do things with us, you act as if you think we're silly."

I do? Caroline wondered. A flush warmed her cheeks. Was it possible that she might have hurt the other girls' feelings in much the same way that they'd hurt hers? "I don't think you're silly," Caroline said. "I just wanted us to have some fun together outdoors."

She looked at Rhonda. "I gave you those beautiful skates for Christmas, and you didn't even want to try them."

"I'd already told you that I didn't *like* skating," Rhonda said quietly. "Those skates weren't a gift to me, Caroline. They were a gift you gave yourself."

Caroline stared at her friend. What an awful thing to say! *But ... it's true,* she realized. She blew out a long breath before admitting, "You're right."

Rhonda squeezed Caroline's hand. "I'm sorry that I hurt your feelings. I never meant to."

"I'm sorry, too," Lydia said quickly.

Caroline felt as if a heavy block of ice had just slipped from her shoulders. "And I am as well," she said. "Now, let's go home."

When the girls got home, Caroline said, "You two go change into dry clothes. I'll be along."

"What are you going to do?" Lydia asked.

"I need to find Grandmother," Caroline told them. "I have some explaining to do."

It was hard to confess to Grandmother. Caroline ended the tale by saying, "I'm sorry, Grandmother. *Very* sorry." She stood with her back to the hearth. The fire's warmth was lovely. The hard look in Grandmother's eyes was terrible.

"What are you sorry about?" Grandmother asked.

Everything! Caroline started to say, but she realized that Grandmother expected something more. "I'm sorry I took the rim from your spinning wheel without asking your permission," Caroline began. "And for going out on the ice. And for talking Lydia and Rhonda into going with me."

Grandmother's face did not soften. "You've made a lot of poor decisions, Caroline."

"Yes, ma'am." Caroline stared at the floor. "I didn't even bring back the rim for your spinning wheel," she added miserably.

"Hmm," Grandmother said. "At least you made one good choice. I'd much rather lose the hoop than lose *you*."

Those words made Caroline feel a tiny bit better.

"And we can easily get a new hoop made," Grandmother added. "But, Caroline, you must *never* again let hurt feelings lead you to make foolish— even dangerous—decisions."

"I won't," Caroline promised. She added silently, *And I'll try not to let my feelings get hurt so easily.* What was done couldn't be undone, but from now on she'd try to consider *other* people's feelings, too.

Thinking about that, Caroline looked away and

noticed Amelia standing by the window, watching some boys passing by with their sleds. She had a look of longing on her face.

"Amelia," Caroline said, "would you like me to take you outside? I could pull you around on my sled."

Amelia stared at her with surprise. "Oh, yes!"

Grandmother gave Caroline a tiny nod of approval.

Five minutes later, Caroline began towing Amelia across the garden on her sled. The little girl clapped her hands and giggled with delight. "This is fun!"

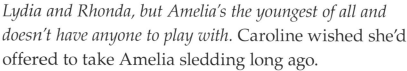

Caroline thought, *I get frustrated because I'm younger than Lydia and Rhonda, but Amelia's the youngest of all and doesn't have anyone to play with.* Caroline wished she'd offered to take Amelia sledding long ago.

"There's a little hill behind the neighbors' house," Caroline called over her shoulder. "They won't mind if we sled there. Would you like to try that?"

"Let's *go!*" Amelia shouted.

Caroline smiled. Perhaps she'd found a friend for outdoor adventures—at least small ones—after all.

New Year's Day—January 1, 1813—dawned
clear and cold. After breakfast Caroline went into
the parlor and sat by the map she'd stitched for Papa.
Where was he, right this minute? Was he somewhere
represented on her map, or had the British taken
him far, far away? *It's a brand-new year, Papa,* Caroline
thought. Surely he would come home in 1813. He
simply *had* to.

Lydia poked her head through the door. "I've
been looking for you, Caroline," she said. "Would
you like to go skating? Just you and me."

Caroline stared at her cousin. "But . . . won't
Rhonda feel left out?" she asked.

"We three don't have to do everything together,"
Lydia said. Her eyes twinkled. "Rhonda won't mind,
I promise."

"Then yes!" Caroline agreed. She raced for the
door but then skidded to a halt. "Would you mind
if we invite Amelia? She can wear the skates I used
when I was little."

Lydia nodded. "That's a fine idea."

Amelia thought that was a fine idea, too. "You'll take *me*?" she squealed. "Thank you!"

Soon Caroline, Lydia, and Amelia had bundled into their warmest clothes and set off for the lake. When Amelia saw other skaters gliding this way and that, she jumped up and down with excitement.

Caroline laughed. "You'll have to stand still long enough for us to put on your skates, Amelia."

The two older girls put on their own skates before strapping the smallest pair onto Amelia's boots. "Caroline and I will hold you up," Lydia promised. "Let us pull you along at first, so you get the feel of the ice."

"We'll stay off to one side, where there are fewer people," Caroline added.

Amelia held herself stiffly at first, but she relaxed as the older girls pulled her along. Soon Lydia said, "Try taking some little strokes. Watch my feet. See how I push off against the ice?"

Caroline felt Amelia's hand squeezing hers even tighter as the little girl tried to copy Lydia's movements. "That's it!" Caroline cried. "You're skating!" Amelia nodded proudly.

Then Caroline heard a familiar voice.

"My goodness!" Rhonda called. "I didn't expect to see my little sister learning to skate today too!"

Caroline whipped her head around. What she saw made her dig one skate blade into the ice and come to a quick halt. She stared, open-mouthed with surprise. Lydia laughed with delight.

Rhonda, wearing her new skates, wobbled to a stop nearby. She was pushing a small chair sled. Grandmother sat in the chair, wrapped in blankets. Her face was glowing.

"I got the idea that day I came out on the ice with you," Rhonda told Caroline. "With your mother's permission, Lydia and I asked Mr. Tate if he'd allow a couple of the shipyard workers to make this chair sled. The handles are nice and strong. As long as I hold on to them, I won't fall down."

"And I," Grandmother added, "am out on the ice for the first time in years!"

"It's a *wonderful* idea," Caroline said.

Amelia tugged Caroline's hand. "I want to ride in the sled."

"Come sit on my lap, child," Grandmother offered. Lydia and Caroline helped Amelia get settled. Grandmother arranged the blankets so that they covered them both.

With a look of determination, Rhonda began skating again, pushing the sled in front of her. "Have fun," she called to Lydia and Caroline. "Soon I'll be able to keep up with you!"

Caroline waved them away with a smile. Somehow, despite the terrible mistakes she'd made recently, everything had turned out well. *Maybe staying steady doesn't mean never making mistakes*, she thought. Maybe the most important thing was to try to learn from mistakes, and do better next time.

"Come on, Caroline," Lydia called. "I'll race you!"

Caroline grinned. "Let's *go!*" she shouted, and pushed off as hard as she could. She marveled at the beauty of sunlight glittering on the snowy shore. She breathed in the crisp, clean air. And soon she was flying over the frozen lake, free as a bird.

LOOKING BACK

GROWING UP
IN
1812

A painting of a Massachusetts family in 1800

When Caroline was a girl, young children like her spent almost all of their time close to parents, brothers and sisters, and other family members.

Babies usually slept in their parents' room in a cradle or slatted crib not too different from the ones used today. Even as children began walking and outgrew their cradles, it was rare for them to have a room to themselves as Caroline did. More often, children shared a bed with siblings or their mother, except in the most well-to-do families. Sharing a bed was such a normal thing to do that many children would have felt odd or even scared if they had to sleep alone.

A baby's cradle

Still, babies in Caroline's time were not coddled. Doctors and other experts believed that children would grow up stronger and healthier if they were "toughened up" as infants. Babies, they said, should not be dressed in heavy or overly warm clothing. They should be allowed to move freely, rather than being swaddled tightly in blankets or squeezed into corsets as babies had been in earlier times. Also, the experts said, daily baths were good for babies—but only if the water was cold. *Brrr!*

When they reached school age, most children spent just a few weeks or months in a classroom each year— if they went to school at all. Many children, especially in rural areas or on the frontier, were too busy helping their parents with farming or housework to attend school. New settlements, like Sackets Harbor, often were simply too small even to have a schoolhouse.

That didn't stop children from learning. Some learned to read, write, and do arithmetic at makeshift schools in nearby houses. Many other children, like Caroline, were schooled by their mothers. There were few textbooks, and it was rare to have paper or anything to write with. Instead, children had to memorize what adults told them and then repeat it back—over and over

Children taking lessons at a neighbor's house because there was no school nearby

A mother teaching her child to read

again. Adults didn't try to make lessons fun or interesting the way teachers do today!

The most important lessons took place at home as part of everyday life. This is how children learned the skills they would need later in life to survive and provide for families of their own. Working alongside their fathers,

A boy often learned a trade such as furniture making from his father.

boys learned to tend animals, chop wood, and plant crops. They also learned the skills needed for the family business, such as shipbuilding, printing, glassblowing, or farming. Working beside their mothers, girls learned to care for younger children, grow food, cook, weave cloth, and sew clothes. By age ten, a girl might well be able to build a cooking fire, bake biscuits, mend clothes, and even care for a sick relative, all on her own.

Stitching samplers taught girls their letters and numbers as well as embroidery stitches.

Embroidery was considered an important skill for girls. Some girls, like Caroline, enjoyed this work. Others, like ten-year-old Patty Polk of Maryland, found the work fussy and boring. Her sampler read: "Patty Polk did this and she hated every stitch she did in it. She loves to read much more."

When it was finally time for play, boys and girls usually played separately. Like the work they did, boys' and girls' games were very different. Boys swam, raced, jumped rope, and played ball. Girls were encouraged to play more quietly. Their games often involved pretending to do the same chores their mothers did every day.

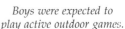

Boys were expected to play active outdoor games.

Young girls practiced weaving bits of straw, made pies out of mud, and watched carefully over their dolls. Children like Caroline might have had one or two homemade toys, such as a doll, a jump rope, or an animal whittled from wood.

A girl playing with a doll at her mother's knee

Neighbors celebrating Christmas Eve with a frosty sleigh ride

Any book was a treasured possession. But children's books were not imaginative and exciting. Mostly, the stories contained lessons adults wanted children to learn about honesty, good manners, and, of course, hard work.

During Caroline's time, Christmas was celebrated in many different ways. In the South, families often enjoyed many days of merriment, including parties with fancy foods, dancing, and music. In the North, where Caroline lived, the holiday was usually quieter. Some people believed that Christmas should be a day for church or prayer, and they did not exchange gifts or celebrate at all. Families who did "keep Christmas" usually marked the day with simple decorations and handmade gifts like the ones Caroline helped make. Families might gather for a special meal with cake or other treats, some hymn singing, and perhaps a visit with nearby relatives. In this way, December 25 was not too different from the way children spent the rest of their time—at home, in the company of parents and the people they knew best.

A SNEAK PEEK AT

Caroline

TAKES A CHANCE

While Caroline is out fishing, she catches sight of an enemy warship—and it's chasing a desperately needed American supply boat. Caroline isn't sure she can stop the British, but she's determined to try!

As the skiff traveled farther along the lakeshore, Caroline watched for familiar landmarks. "There!" she announced. "See that marshy area ahead, Rhonda?" She pointed to a swampy cove where tall grasses and cattails pushed from the water. The shoreline was wooded, with no houses in sight. "That's where Hickory Creek flows into the lake."

Seth began expertly rowing through the grasses. Several ducks launched into the air, scolding Caroline and her friends with noisy *quack-quack-quack*s as they flew away.

"Why is this a good fishing spot?" Rhonda asked.

"Two reasons," Caroline told her. "First, fish like the warmer water flowing from the creek."

"And in just a moment, you'll see the second reason we like this spot," Seth promised.

The skiff swished through clumps of cattails. Caroline reached out to touch the leaves as they passed. She liked the way they felt in her fingers, smooth and firm. Then the skiff gently came to a stop. Beneath them, the hull made a soft scraping sound.

Rhonda looked alarmed. "Have we run aground?"

"We're on a sandbar," Caroline explained. "Look into the water. See?" The skiff rested on a long mound of sand and gravel just underwater. "It's an easy place for us to stop and fish."

"Will it take long to catch a fish?" Rhonda asked.

"Not if we're lucky!" Caroline said cheerfully. She felt lucky today. The sun was shining, the air felt warm, and she and her friends were on a fishing trip!

Seth handed each of the girls a fishing pole. A string dangled from each pole, with a wire hook on the end. Then he reached for the tin pail that held the worms.

Rhonda's nose wrinkled. "Will I have to put a worm on the hook myself?"

"Only if you want to be allowed to eat whatever you catch," Caroline teased.

"I'll do the worm for you," Seth told Rhonda.

When he had finished, Caroline showed Rhonda how to cast the hook into the water. "And now, wait until you feel a tug on the line," she explained. "That's how you know you have a fish."

"Will it take long to catch a fish?" Rhonda asked.
"Not if we're lucky!" Caroline said cheerfully. She felt lucky today.

"I hope I catch—" Rhonda stopped suddenly. "Oh, look!" She pointed at a long, low boat that had just come into view. An American flag fluttered from the bateau's single mast. The boat was traveling near the shore, heading toward Sackets Harbor. Rhonda's eyes lit up. "Maybe the American soldiers are returning!"

Seth shook his head. "I don't think so. Since it's by itself, it's most likely a supply boat."

Caroline's hopes soared like a gull. She held her breath, squinting at the bateau until she was able to pick out the red banner flying below the national flag. "It's Irish Jack!" she cried.

"Hurrah!" Rhonda cheered.

"Jack and his men will easily make Sackets Harbor with plenty of time to unload yet today," Seth said. "Watch out, Rhonda, I think your line got tangled in those cattails..." His voice trailed away. "Oh no," he whispered. He pointed straight north, past the marsh to Lake Ontario's open water.

Caroline's heart dropped as she followed his gaze. A sloop had just appeared, and she could see a British flag flying from its tallest mast. "It's an enemy ship," she whispered.

Rhonda's eyes were wide. "It's making straight for us!"

"It's not making straight for *us*," Seth said grimly. "It's making straight for the bateau."

Her heart racing, Caroline eyed the sloop. Seth was right. Although the British sloop was zigzagging to make best use of the wind, its captain was clearly heading toward the American supply boat.

Irish Jack must have seen the enemy sloop, too. His bateau was moving quickly now. It had drawn so close to the marsh that Caroline could see Irish Jack's wild red hair. His crewmen were pulling hard at the oars.

Caroline clenched handfuls of skirt fabric in her fists. "Faster!" she urged the crew.

"Are they trying to run for Sackets Harbor?" Rhonda asked. "Why don't they raise their sail?"

"The wind's against them," Caroline told her. She felt hot inside. "All they can do is row."

"Those blasted British!" Seth said angrily. "I wish I could drive them back to Upper Canada myself!"

Caroline felt the same way. "At least the bateau is close enough to shore that the men can jump off and slip away into the woods. They won't be taken prisoner." That thought gave her a scrap of comfort, but she hated to think of the British capturing the bateau and its precious supplies.

READ ALL OF CAROLINE'S STORIES,
available at bookstores and *americangirl.com.*

MEET CAROLINE
When the British attack Caroline's village, she
makes a daring choice that helps to win the day.

CAROLINE'S SECRET MESSAGE
Caroline and Mama take a dangerous journey
to the British fort where Papa is held prisoner.

A SURPRISE FOR CAROLINE
Caroline finds herself on thin ice after
friendship troubles lead to a bad decision.

CAROLINE TAKES A CHANCE
When a warship threatens American supplies,
can Caroline's little fishing boat turn it away?

CAROLINE'S BATTLE
As a battle rages right in her own village,
Caroline faces a terrible choice.

CHANGES FOR CAROLINE
Caroline pitches in on her cousin's new farm—
and comes home to a wonderful surprise.